THE WRECK OF THE ZANZIBAR

Also by Michael Morpurgo

Arthur: High King of Britain
Escape From Shangri-La
Friend or Foe
The Ghost of Grania O'Malley
Kensuke's Kingdom
King of the Cloud Forests
Little Foxes
Long Way Home
Mr Nobody's Eyes
My Friend Walter
The Sleeping Sword
Twist of Gold
Waiting for Anya
War Horse
The War of Jenkins' Ear
The White Horse of Zennor
Why the Whales Came

For younger readers

Colly's Barn
Conker
Little Foxes
The Marble Crusher
The Nine Lives of Montezuma
The Sandman and the Turtles

Edited by Michael Morpurgo

Muck and Magic: Stories from the Countryside
More Muck and Magic

MICHAEL MORPURGO

THE WRECK OF THE ZANZIBAR

ILLUSTRATED BY CHRISTIAN BIRMINGHAM

EGMONT

First published in Great Britain 1995
Reissued 2003
by Egmont Books Limited
239 Kensington High Street, London W8 6SA

ISBN 1 4052 0930 5

5 7 9 10 8 6 4

A CIP catalogue record for this title is available from the British Library

Typeset by Avon DataSet Ltd
Printed and bound in Great Britain by the CPI Group

To Marion, Keith, Daniel and Charlie

Hell Bay
Scilly Rock
Popplestones
BRYHER
Gweal
TRESCO
Great Porth
Merrick Island
Seal Rock
Samson Hill
Rushy Bay
Illiswilgig
Tearing Ledges
Puffin Island
Mincarlo
White Island
Green Island
SAMSON
NORTH WEST PASSAGE
Great Minalto
ST. MARY'S SOUND
Annet
ST. AGNES
Gugh

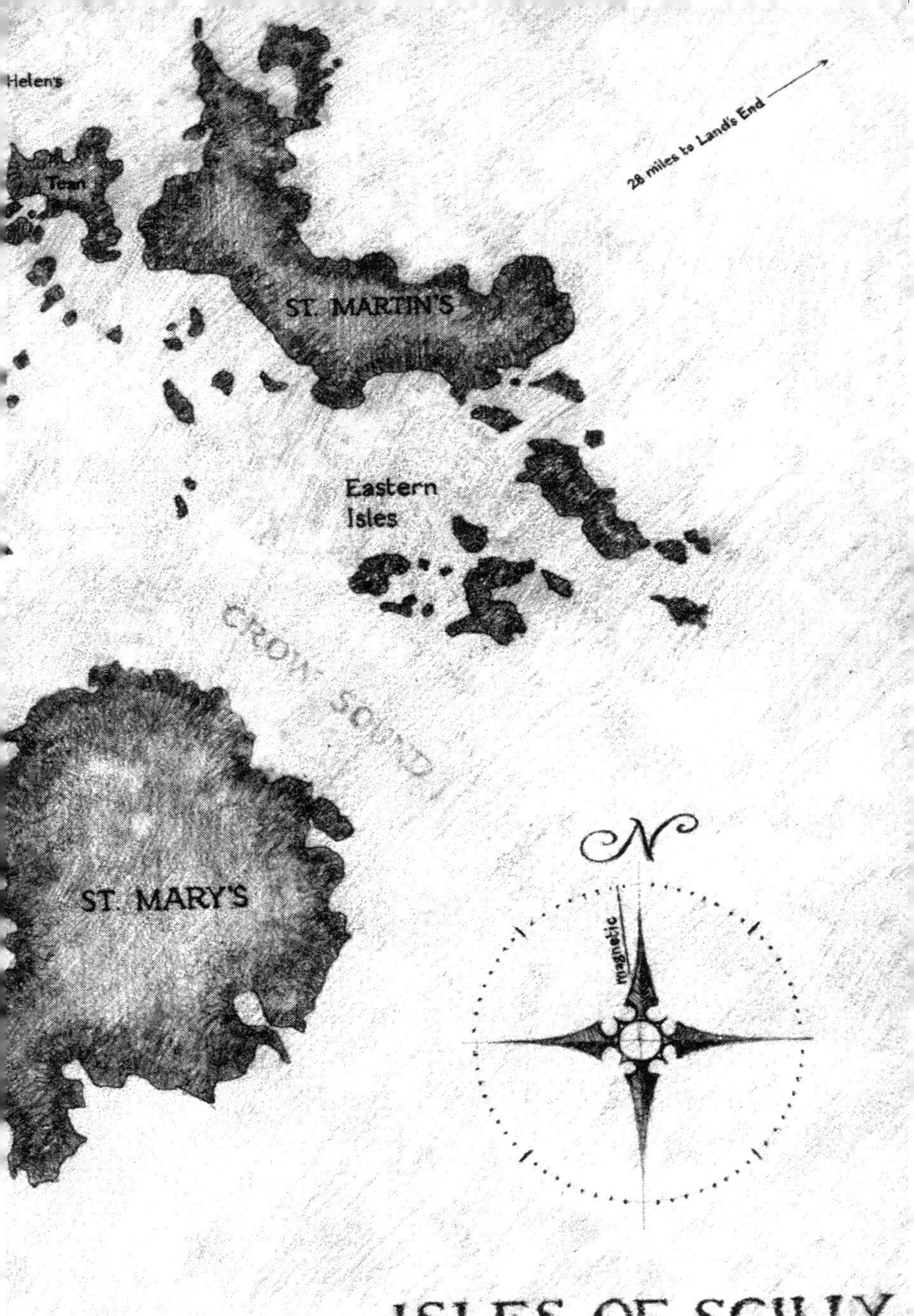

ISLES OF SCILLY

GREAT-AUNT LAURA

MY GREAT-AUNT LAURA DIED A FEW MONTHS ago. She was a hundred years old. She had her cocoa last thing at night, as she usually did, put the cat out, went to sleep and never woke up. There's not a better way to die.

I took the boat across to Scilly for the funeral – almost everyone in the family did. I met again cousins and aunts and uncles I hardly recognised, and who hardly recognised me. The little church on Bryher was packed, standing room only. Everyone on Bryher was there, and they came from all over the Scilly Isles, from St Mary's, St Martin's, St Agnes and Tresco.

We sang the hymns lustily because we knew

Great-aunt Laura would enjoy a rousing send-off. Afterwards we had a family gathering in her tiny cottage overlooking Stinking Porth Bay. There was tea and crusty brown bread and honey. I took one mouthful and I was a child again. Wanting to be on my own, I went up the narrow stairs to the room that had been mine when I came every summer for my holidays. The same oil lamp was by the bed, the same peeling wallpaper, the same faded curtains with the red sailing boats dipping through the waves.

I sat down on the bed and closed my eyes. I was eight years old again and ahead of me were two weeks of sand and sea and boats and shrimping, and oystercatchers and gannets, and Great-aunt Laura's stories every night before she drew the curtains against the moon and left me alone in my bed.

Someone called from downstairs and I was back to now.

Everyone was crowded into her sittingroom. There was a cardboard box open in the middle of the floor.

'Ah, there you are, Michael,' said Uncle Will. He was a little irritated, I thought.

'We'll begin then.'

And a hush fell around the room. He dipped into

the box and held up a parcel.

'It looks as if she's left us one each,' said Uncle Will. Every parcel was wrapped in old newspaper and tied with string, and there was a large brown label attached to each one. Uncle Will read out the names. I had to wait some minutes for mine. There was nothing I particularly wanted, except Zanzibar of course, but then everyone wanted Zanzibar. Uncle Will was waving a parcel at me.

'Michael,' he said, 'here's yours.'

I took it upstairs and unwrapped it sitting on the bed. It felt like a book of some sort, and so it was, but not a printed book. It was handmade, handwritten in pencil, the pages sewn together. The title on the cover read *The Diary of Laura Perryman* and there was a watercolour painting on the cover of a four-masted ship keeling over in a storm and heading for the rocks. With the book there was an envelope.

I opened it and read.

Dear Michael

When you were little I told you lots and lots of stories about Bryher, about the Isles of Scilly. You know about the ghosts on Samson, about the bell that rings under the sea off St Martin's, about King Arthur still waiting in his cave under the Eastern Isles.

You remember? Well, here is my story, the story of me and my twin brother Billy whom you never knew. How I wish you had. It is a true story and I did not want it to die with me.

When I was young I kept a diary, not an everyday diary. I didn't write in it very often, just whenever I felt like it. Most of it isn't worth the reading and I've already thrown it away - I've lived an ordinary sort of life. But for a few months a long, long time ago, my life was not ordinary at all. This is the diary of those few months.

Do you remember you always used to ask where Zanzibar came from? (You called him 'Marzipan' when you were small.) I never told you, did I? I never told anyone. Well, now you'll find out at last.

Goodbye, dear Michael, and God bless you.

Your Great-aunt Laura

P.S. I hope you like my little sketches. I'm a better artist than I am a writer, I think. When I come back in my next life - and I shall - I shall be a great artist. I've promised myself.

The Diary of Laura Perryman

(1907)

JANUARY 20TH

'LAURA PERRYMAN, YOU ARE FOURTEEN YEARS old today.'

I said that to the mirror this morning when I wished myself 'Happy Birthday'. Sometimes, like this morning, I don't much want to be Laura Perryman, who's lived on Bryher all her life and milks cows. I want to be Lady Eugenia Fitzherbert with long red hair and green eyes, who wears a big wide hat with a white ostrich feather and who travels the world in steamships with four funnels. But then, I also want to be Billy Perryman so I can row out in the gig and build boats and run fast. Billy's fourteen too – being my twin brother, he would be. But I'm not Lady Eugenia Fitzherbert, whoever she is, and I'm not Billy; I'm me. I'm Laura Perryman and I'm fourteen years old today.

Everyone is pleased with me, even Father, because I was the one who spotted the ship before they did on St Mary's. It was just that I was in the right place at the right time, that's all. I'd been milking the cows with Billy, as usual, and I was coming back with the buckets over Watch Hill when I saw sails on

the horizon out beyond White Island. It looked like a schooner, three-masted. We left the buckets and ran all the way home.

The gig was launched in five minutes. I watched the whole thing from the top of Samson Hill with everyone else. We saw the St Mary's gig clear the harbour wall, the wind and the tide in her favour. The race was on. For some time it looked as if the St Mary's gig would reach the schooner first, as she so

often does, but we found clear water and a fair wind out beyond Samson and we were flying along. I could see the chief holding on to the mast, and Billy and Father pulling side by side in the middle of the boat. How I wanted to be one of them, to be out there rowing with them. I can handle an oar as well as Billy. He knows it, everyone knows it. But the chief won't hear of it - and he's the coxswain - and neither will Father. They think that's an end of it. But it isn't. One day, one day . . . Anyway today we won the race, so I should be pleased about that, I suppose.

The St Mary's boat lost an oar. She was left dead in the water and had to turn back. We watched our gig draw alongside the schooner and we all cheered till we were hoarse. Through the telescope I could see the chief climbing up the ladder to pilot the schooner into St Mary's. I could see them helping him on board, then shaking hands with him. He took off his cap and waved and we all cheered again. It would mean money for everyone, and there's precious little of that around. When the gig came back into Great Porth we were all there to meet her. We helped haul her up the beach. She's always lighter when we've won. Father hugged me and Billy winked at me. It's an American ship, he says, the *General Lee,* bound for New York. She'll be tied up in St Mary's for repairs to her mizzenmast and could be there a week, maybe more.

This evening, Billy and I had our birthday cake from Granny May as usual. The chief and crew were all there as well, so the cake didn't last long. They sang 'Happy Birthday' to us and then the chief said we were all a little less poor because Laura Perryman had spotted the *General Lee.* And I felt good. They were all smiling at me. Now's the time, I thought, I'll ask them again.

'Can I row with Billy in the gig?'

They all laughed and said what they always said, that girls don't row in gigs. They never had.

I went to the hen-house and cried. It's the only place I can cry in peace. And then Granny May came in with the last piece of cake and said there are plenty of things that women can do, that men can't. It doesn't seem that way to me. I want to row in that gig, and I will. One day I will.

Billy came into my room just now. He's had another argument with Father – this time the milk buckets weren't clean enough. There's always something, and Father will shout at him so. Billy says he wants to go to America and that one day he will. He's always saying things like that. I wish he wouldn't. It frightens me. I wish Father would be kinder to him.

FEBRUARY 12TH
The Night of the Storm

A TERRIBLE STORM LAST NIGHT AND THE PINE tree at the bottom of the garden came down, missing the hen-house by a whisker. The wind was so loud we never even heard it fall. I'm sure the hens did. We've lost more slates off the roof above Billy's room. But we were lucky. The end of Granny May's roof has gone completely. It just lifted off in the night. It's sitting lopsided across her escallonia hedge. Father's been up there all day trying to do what he can to keep the rain out. Everyone would be there helping, but there isn't a building on the island that hasn't been battered. Granny May just sat down in her kitchen all day and shook her head. She wouldn't come away. She kept saying she'll never be able to pay for a new roof and where will she go and what will she do? We stayed with her, Mother and me, giving her cups of tea and telling her it will be all right.

'Something'll turn up,' Mother said. She's always saying that. When Father gets all inside himself and miserable and silent, when the cows aren't milking well, when he can't afford the timber to build his boats, she always says, 'Don't worry, something'll turn up.'

She never says it to me because she knows I won't believe her. I won't believe her because I know she doesn't believe it herself. She just says it to make him feel better. She just hopes it'll come true. Still, it must have made Granny May feel better. She was her old self again this evening, talking away happily to herself. Everyone on the island calls her a mad old stick. But she's not really mad. She's just old and a bit forgetful. She does talk to herself, but then she's lived alone most of her life, so it's not surprising really. I love her because she's my granny, because she loves me, and because she shows it. Mother has persuaded her to come and stay for a bit until she can move back into her house again.

Billy's in trouble again. He went off to St Mary's without telling anyone. He was gone all day. When he got back this evening he never said a word to me or Granny May. Father buttoned his lip for as long as he could. It's always been the same with Father and Billy. They set each other off. They always have. It's Billy's fault really, most of the time anyway. He starts it. He does things without thinking. He says things without thinking. And Father's like a squall. He seems calm and quiet one moment and then . . . I could feel it coming. He banged the table and shouted. Billy had no right going off like that, he said, when there was so much to be put right at Granny May's. Billy told him he'd do what he pleased, when he pleased and he wasn't anyone's slave. Then he got up from the table and ran out, slamming the door behind him. Mother went after him. Poor Mother, always the peacemaker.

Father and Granny May had a good long talk about 'young folk today', and how they don't know how lucky they are these days and how they don't know what hard work is all about. They're still at it downstairs. I went in to see Billy just a few minutes ago. He's been crying, I can tell. He says he doesn't want to talk. He's thinking, he says. That makes a change, I suppose.

FEBRUARY 14TH

GRANNY MAY'S ROOF HAS BEEN PATCHED UP. She moved back home yesterday. We are on our own again.

Father said at breakfast he thought Molly would calve down today and that Billy and me should keep an eye on her. Billy went off to St Mary's and I went up to check Molly this afternoon on my own. She was lying down by the hedge, her calf curled up beside her. He looked as if he was sleeping at first, but he wasn't. There were flies on his face and his eyes weren't blinking. He was dead, and I couldn't make Molly get up. I pushed her and pushed her, but she wouldn't move. I didn't tell Father because I knew how angry he'd be. We should have been there, Billy or me - one of us should have been there. I fetched Mother instead. She couldn't get Molly on her feet either, so in the end we had to call Father from the boatshed. He tried everything, but Molly just laid her head down on the grass and died.

Father sat beside her, stroked her neck and said nothing. But I knew what he was thinking. We only had four cows and we'd just lost the best of them. Then he looked up and said, 'Where's that boy?'

Mother tried to comfort him, but he wouldn't even answer her.

'Just you wait till he gets back, just you wait.' That was all he said.

Billy came back at sundown. I saw him come sailing up Tresco Channel. I ran down to Green Bay to tell him about Molly, to warn him about Father. Then I saw that he was not alone.

'This is Joseph Hannibal,' said Billy. 'He's American, off the *General Lee* in St Mary's.'

Joseph Hannibal is a bear of a man with a bushy black beard and twitchy eyebrows that meet in the middle so he always looks angry. I never had a chance to tell Billy about Molly. He'd brought Joseph

Hannibal back to see the island, he said, and they went off together up towards Hell Bay.

I didn't see them again until supper. Father sat in a stony silence and Mother smiled all the time, thinly, like she does when she is worried. But after a time she was doing what I was doing, what Billy was doing, what even Father was doing. We were all listening to Joseph Hannibal.

He's been all over the world, the South Sea Islands, Australia, Japan, China, the frozen North. He's sailed on tea clippers, on steamships, and he's been whaling too.

'Yessir,' he went on, puffing at his pipe, 'I've seen whales longer than this entire house and that's the honest truth.'

You had to listen to him - I mean, you wanted to listen. You wanted him to go on all night. Then Mother said we should go up to bed - that we had the cows to milk early in the morning. Billy said he wasn't tired, that he'd be up later. He stayed where he was. Father looked at him hard, but Billy didn't seem to notice. He had eyes only for Joseph Hannibal.

He still doesn't know about Molly, and he's still down there now talking to Joseph Hannibal.

There's something about Joseph Hannibal, something I don't like, but I'm not sure what it is. One thing I am sure of though. As soon as he's gone Father's going to have something to say, and when he does I wouldn't want to be in Billy's shoes.

I'm trying to stay awake by writing this, so I can warn him about Molly, but my eyes are pricking and I can hardly keep them open.

FEBRUARY 15TH

THIS IS THE WORST DAY OF MY WHOLE LIFE. IT began well. Joseph Hannibal left the house this morning at last. I thought he'd sail away on the evening tide and that would be the end of him. I was wrong. Billy has gone with him. Even as I write it, I can hardly believe it. Billy has gone.

It all began just after Joseph Hannibal left. We've had arguments before, Billy and me, but never like this. He didn't seem a bit sad when I told him, at last, about Molly and her calf. He just said that I should have been there, or Mother; that it wasn't his fault. I got angry and shouted at him. Billy just shrugged and walked off. I hate it when he does that. I raced after him and grabbed him. He turned on me and told me I was taking Father's side against him. I knew then that it was all because of Joseph Hannibal. It's as if he's split us apart. Billy thinks that everything about him is wonderful, that he's doing what a proper man should. He won't hear a word against him.

This afternoon Billy and Father had their expected set-to about Molly. Father roared and of course Billy shouted back at him. He wasn't going to stay and be a cowman all his life, he had better things to be doing. I've never seen Billy like it. The angrier he became, the more he seemed to grow. Nose to nose in the kitchen he was as big as Father. Father said he'd strap him if he didn't hold his tongue and Billy just stared at him and said nothing, his eyes like steel. Mother came between them and Billy stormed out. I followed him.

We went to Rushy Bay where we always go to talk when we don't want anyone else to hear. We sat on the sand together, and that was when he told me. He'd been talking to Joseph Hannibal. Joseph Hannibal had asked the skipper of the General Lee and the skipper had agreed: Billy could join the ship as cabin boy.

'I'm going, Laura,' Billy said. 'I was thinking about it all last night. And not just because of Father, either. It's a big world out there and I'm going to see it. This could be my only chance.'

And I could see that he meant it, that I couldn't argue him round. I tried all the same. I begged him to stay. I even said I'd go with him. He shook his head and looked away. I know Billy so well, better than he knows me, I think. Once he's made up his mind there's no stopping him. I knew it was hopeless.

He put his arm around me and told me he was sorry, that I'd be all right. He'd write to me, and when he comes back he's going to bring me lots of things from America, from China, from the frozen North. When I cried he hugged me very tight and said he'd go now, just as he was. He didn't want to have to go home again.

'You'll tell Mother?' he said. 'You'll say goodbye for me?'

I walked in silence with him down past the church to the quay. We saw Father paring a hedge up in the field where Molly had died. Billy looked at him and said nothing. He was close to tears. He turned away.

'And say goodbye to Granny May too,' he said. From the quayside we looked across at St Mary's. We could see the masts of the General Lee.

'She's a fine ship,' he said. 'A fast ship. She'll take me all over the world, Joseph Hannibal said.'

He smoothed my hair and told me to go home without looking back. I cried all the way home, not so much because Billy was gone and I might never see him again, but because he didn't want me to go with him.

This evening, from the top of Samson Hill, I watched the General Lee sail out past St Agnes. Billy was right. She was a fine ship. I knew he'd be looking back at Bryher and he knew I'd be up on Samson Hill. I could feel his eyes on me. I shivered, not from cold, but because I knew then as I know now, that I'll never see Billy again. Her sails were red in the last of the sun, as red as any blood.

I said nothing till just before supper, when Mother asked where Billy was. I told her as gently as I knew how. She sat down and her eyes were suddenly empty of life.

'No,' she whispered. And that was all.

Father was working late in the boathouse. He came in a few minutes ago. I was sitting on the stairs

when she told him.

'You drove him away,' she said, shaking her head. 'You shouldn't have. You shouldn't have.'

'He'll be back,' said Father. 'You'll see.'

Mother turned away from him. She didn't believe him, and neither do I.

JULY 21ST

MY HOUSE IS NOT MY HOME ANY MORE. IT'S A place I live in. My island is a prison and I am quite alone. Mother and Father are strangers to each other. Billy has been gone for over four months now. There's been no letter, no word. We scarcely ever speak of him. It's as if he never lived.

I went to his room this morning and found Mother sitting on his bed staring at the wall, rocking back and forth. She had his blue jersey on her lap. I went and sat beside her. She tried to smile but couldn't. She hasn't smiled since Billy left.

I do the morning milking on my own now. That's when I most miss Billy. I talk to the cows and they listen. Maybe they understand too - I hope so. They're not milking at all well - I think perhaps they're missing Billy, like everyone else. They aren't eating properly either. Their coats are staring, and they're not licking themselves. They're just not how they should be.

JULY 30TH

IN CHURCH TODAY I WAS LISTENING TO THE vicar. It was as if he was speaking just to me. He said we mustn't hope for anything at all in this life, only in the next life. I think I understand what he means. You only get disappointed if you hope.

Every night – like tonight, when I've finished this – I lie in the darkness and hope and pray that Billy will come back. I pray out loud, just in case God can't hear me hoping. And every morning, as soon as I wake up, I go to the window and hope to see him running up the path. But each day he isn't there makes even hoping more hopeless.

JULY 31ST

EVEN MY OTHER HOPE HAS COME TO NOTHING. I hoped that, with Billy gone, I might at last be allowed to take his place in the gig. I finally plucked up courage enough to ask the chief. He said I had to ask Father. I waited until he was doing the evening milking – he's always gentler when he's up with the cows. He was with Rosie in the barn.

'There's something wrong with these cows,' he said, without looking up.

'Hardly a bucketful between the lot of them. They go on like this, we're in real trouble, real trouble. They've not been right, none of them, not since Billy left, none of us have.'

His eyes were filled with tears when he looked up at me. 'Mother's right,' he said. 'It was my fault Billy went away.'

'No it wasn't,' I said. 'It was Joseph Hannibal.' It was only half the truth, and Father knew it. He went back to his milking.

I asked him then what I had come to ask him. I knew I shouldn't but I had to. He was on his feet at once shouting at me. Rosie kicked out in alarm and the bucket went over.

'Is that all you ever think about?' he roared. 'Your brother's run off to sea. Every cow I've got is sick. It's these cows put food in your belly, girl, you know that?' I knew that. Of course I knew that. 'They die. We die. They're all we've got. And you come fussing to me about the gig. How many times have I told you? There's never been a girl rowed out in the gig, not on this island, not on any island. And you'll not be the first, do you hear me?'

I ran off with him still shouting after me. I never thought I could think it. I never thought I could write it, but I hate my father.

AUGUST 23RD

ROSIE IS VERY SICK. THERE'S NO DOUBT ABOUT it now. She's thinner every day. She's stopped milking entirely. We sell what we can - a little to everyone. Until now the cows always made enough milk for the whole island. We're the only people with milking cows. They rely on us for their milk - they always have done. Now with Molly gone and Rosie poorly we just haven't got enough to go around. We've still got Celandine and Petal, but Petal's not in milk and Celandine's giving precious little. Father says if anything happens to either of them we're done for. All we can do, he says, is to hope and pray for a wreck. So that's what I'm doing, hoping and praying for a wreck.

I long for Mother to tell me that everything will be all right, even if she doesn't mean it. But she's stopped saying anything. I think maybe she's dying inside.

I went to the top of Samson Hill this evening and looked out to the open sea. There was a big swell building, and the sky was very low and grey over the sea.

I tried to make my eyes see over the horizon as far as America. It's the closest I can get to Billy. He was out there somewhere on that sea. I could feel it. I could feel he was still alive and I was suddenly happy in spite of everything. I just wish he would come back home. If only he would, then everything would be all right again. I'm sure of it.

SEPTEMBER 6TH

A GREAT STORM IS GATHERING, THE SEAS huge, the skies full of anger.

We went to fetch Granny May this morning. Her roof looks as if it might blow off at any time. She didn't want to leave, she didn't want to be a trouble. Mother paid her no heed and we took an arm each and brought her home.

All day we huddled together around the fire in the kitchen trying not to listen to the howling outside. Father saw to the cows today. He's shut them in the shed now, out of the storm.

It's a high tide tonight. Father says there'll be flooding. The sea will pour in across from Great Porth and make another island of us – it's happened before.

On nights like this, when I was little, I used to go into Billy's room, climb into his bed and we'd talk till morning. We could pretend we weren't frightened and if we pretended hard enough, then we weren't.

Now I sit alone on my bed and listen to the roar of the storm outside and the whistle of the wind in the windows and I am afraid. I can only think of all that sea pounding our little island, trying to suck us down and sink us forever. I am so afraid.

Where are you, Billy? Where are you? Why did you go and leave me?

SEPTEMBER 7TH

THE STORM HAS PASSED, BUT IT HAS RUINED us utterly. I went out early to milk the cows. The meadows were a great lake and the cowshed on the hillside had gone. The gate into the meadows was off its hinges. There were no cows to be seen, not at first. Then I saw them. Celandine and Petal were lying drowned and swollen where the sea had left them, legs stiff in the air. I ran home.

No one would believe me, because they didn't want to believe me. *I* didn't want to believe me. They followed me out. Father knelt beside them in the shallows and sobbed. Granny May and Mother led him home, his head in his hands.

I stroked the white patch on Petal's neck, where I always patted her after milking. She was so cold. Her big, blue eyes gazed up at me, unseeing. I ran off and later found myself outside Granny May's house. Her whole roof had gone this time, but that wasn't all. When I went round the side I saw the end of the cottage had collapsed around the chimney. Next to it the Jenkins' house too was beyond repair, like a giant had trampled all over it.

I walked all around the island. Hardly a house had survived intact. When I got home I found the hen-house gone, the hens with it, and the kitchen window had been blown in.

Several boats, not ours, thank God, have been driven on to the rocks and smashed to pieces, and the chief has lost his crabber altogether. Bryher is wrecked. It's like a nightmare. I want to wake up and find none of it is true. We are all ruined and done for and we shall have to leave. Everyone says so – except Granny May. But she hasn't been told about her house yet. Father won't do it and Mother won't do it. They just can't bring themselves to tell her, and neither can I.

When Granny May had gone up to bed this

evening Father said, 'It's like the beginning of the end. In a few years' time Bryher will be like Samson and Tean, abandoned and deserted, left to the rabbits and the birds.'

He cried and I knew I didn't hate him any more, I knew I loved him still. Mother won't cry. I've never seen Mother cry. She put her arms around Father and held him, and that's the first time she's done that since Billy left.

SEPTEMBER 8TH

TODAY I FOUND A TURTLE. I THINK IT'S CALLED a leatherback turtle. I found one once before, but it was dead. This one has been washed up alive.

Father had sent me down to collect driftwood on Rushy Bay. He said there'd be plenty about after a storm like that. He was right.

I'd been there for half an hour or so heaping up the wood, before I noticed the turtle in the tideline of piled seaweed. I thought at first he was just a washed-up tree stump covered in seaweed.

He was upside down on the sand. I pulled the seaweed off him. His eyes were open, unblinking. He was more dead than alive, I thought. His flippers were quite still, and held out to the clouds above as if he was worshipping them. He was massive, as long as this bed, and wider. He had a face like a two hundred year old man, wizened and wrinkled and wise with a gently-smiling mouth.

I looked around, and there were more gulls gathering. They were silent, watching, waiting; and I knew well enough what they were waiting for. I pulled away more of the seaweed and saw that the gulls had been at him already. There was blood under his neck where the skin had been pecked. I had got there just in time. I bombarded the gulls with pebbles and they flew off protesting noisily, leaving me alone with my turtle.

I knew it would be impossible to roll him over, but I tried anyway. I could rock him back and forth on his shell, but I could not turn him over, no matter how hard I tried. After a while I gave up and sat down beside him on the sand. His eyes kept closing slowly as if he was dropping off to sleep, or maybe he was dying – I couldn't be sure. I stroked him under his chin where I thought he would like it, keeping my hand well away from his mouth.

A great curling stormwave broke and came

tumbling towards us. When it went hissing back over the sand, it left behind a broken spar. It was as if the sea was telling me what to do. I dragged the spar up the beach. Then I saw the turtle's head go back and his eyes closed. I've often seen seabirds like that. Once their heads go back there's nothing you can do. But I couldn't just let him die. I couldn't. I shouted at him. I shook him. I told him he wasn't to die, that I'd turn him over somehow, that it wouldn't be long.

I dug a deep hole in the sand beside him. I would lever him up and topple him in. I drove the spar into the sand underneath his shell. I drove it in again and again, until it was as deep as I could get it. I hauled back on it and felt him shift. I threw all my weight on it and at last he tumbled over into the hole, and the right way up, too. But when I scrambled over to him, his head lay limp in the sand, his eyes closed to the world. There wasn't a flicker of life about him. He was dead. I was quite sure of it now. It's silly, I know - I had only known him for a few minutes - but I felt I had lost a friend.

I made a pillow of soft sea lettuce for his head and knelt beside him. I cried till there were no more tears to cry. And then I saw the gulls were back. They knew too. I screamed at them, but they just glared at me and moved in closer.

'No!' I cried. 'No!'

I would never let them have him, never. I piled a mountain of seaweed on top of him and my driftwood on top of that. The next tide would take him away. I left him and went home.

I went back to Rushy Bay this evening, at high tide, just before nightfall, to see if my turtle was gone. He was still there. The high tide had not been high enough. The gulls were gone though, all of them. I really don't know what made me want to see his face once more. I pulled the wood and seaweed away until I could see the top of his head. As I looked it moved and lifted. He was blinking up at me. He was alive again! I could have kissed him, really I could. But I didn't quite dare.

He's still there now, all covered up against the gulls, I hope. In the morning . . .

I had to stop writing because Father just came in. He hardly ever comes in my room, so I knew at once something was wrong.

'You all right?' he said, standing in the doorway.

'What've you been up to?'

'Nothing,' I said. 'Why?'

'Old man Jenkins. He said he saw you down on Rushy Bay.'

'I was just collecting the wood,' I told him, as calmly as I could, 'like you said I should.' I find lying so difficult. I'm just not good at it.

'He thought you were crying, crying your eyes out, he says.'

'I was not,' I said, but I dared not look at him. I pretended to go on writing in my diary.

'You are telling me the truth, Laura?' He knew I wasn't, he knew it.

'Course,' I said. I just wished he would go.

'What do you find to write in that diary of yours?' he asked.

'Things,' I said. 'Just things.'

And he went out and shut the door behind him. He knows something, but he doesn't know what. I'm going to have to be very careful. If Father finds out about the turtle, I'm in trouble. He's only got to go down to Rushy Bay and look. That turtle would just be food to him, and to anyone else who finds him. We're all hungry, everyone is getting hungrier every day. I should tell him. I know I should. But I can't do it. I just can't let them eat him.

In the morning, early, I'll have to get him back into the sea. I don't know how I'm going to do it, but somehow I will. I must. Now it's not only the gulls I have to save him from.

SEPTEMBER 9TH
The Day of the Turtle

I SHALL REMEMBER TODAY AS LONG AS I LIVE. This morning I slipped away as soon as ever I could. No one saw me go and no one followed me, I made quite sure of that. I'd lain awake most of the night wondering how I was going to get my turtle back into the water. But as I made my way down to Rushy Bay, the morning fog lifting off the sea, I had no idea at all how I would do it. Even as I uncovered him, I still didn't know. I only knew it had to be done. So I talked to him. I was trying to explain it all to him, how he mustn't worry, how I'd find a way, but that I didn't yet know what way. He's got eyes that make you think he understands. Maybe he doesn't, but you never know. Somehow, once I'd started talking, I felt it was rude not to go on. I fetched some seawater in my hat and I poured it over him. He seemed to like it, lifting his head into it as I poured. So I did it again and again. I told him all about the storm, about Granny May's roof, about the

battered boats, and he looked at me. He was listening.

He was so weak though. He kept trying to move, trying to dig his flippers into the sand, but he hadn't the strength to do it. His mouth kept opening and shutting as if he was *gasping* for breath.

Then I had an idea. I scooped out a long deep

channel all the way down to the sea. I would wait for the tide to come in as far as it could, and when the time came I would ease him down into the channel and he could wade out to sea. As I dug I told him my plan. When I'd finished I lay down beside him, exhausted, and waited for the tide.

I told him then all about Billy, about Joseph Hannibal and the *General Lee,* and about how I missed Billy so much, all about the cows dying and about how nothing had gone right since the day Billy left. When I looked across at him his eyes were closed. He seemed to be dozing in the sun. I'd been talking to myself.

The gulls never left us alone, not for a minute. They stood eyeing us from the rocks, from the shallows. When I threw stones at them now, they didn't fly off, they just hopped a little further away, and they always came back. I didn't go home for lunch – I just hoped Father wouldn't come looking for me. I couldn't leave my turtle, not with the gulls all around us just waiting their moment. Besides, the tide was coming in now, closer all the time. Then there was barely five yards of sand left between the sea and my turtle, and the water was washing up the channel just as I'd planned it. It was now or never.

I told him what he had to do.

'You've got to walk the rest,' I said. 'You want to get back in the sea, you've got to walk, you hear me?'

He tried. He honestly tried. Time and again he dug the edge of his flippers into the sand, but he just couldn't move himself.

The flippers dug in again, again, but he stayed where he was. I tried pushing him from behind. That didn't work. I tried moving his flippers for him one by one. That didn't work. I slapped his shell. I shouted at him. All he did was swallow once or twice and blink at me. In the end I tried threatening him. I crouched down in front of him.

'All right,' I said. 'All right. You stay here if you like. See if I care. You see those gulls? You know what they're waiting for? If they don't get you, then someone else'll find you and you'll be turtle stew.' I was shouting at him now. I was really shouting at him. 'Turtle stew, do you hear me!' All the while his eyes never left my face, not for a moment. Bullying hadn't worked either. So now I tried begging.

'Please,' I said, 'please.' But his eyes gave me the answer I already knew. He could not move. He hadn't the strength. There was nothing else left to try. From the look in his eyes I think he knew it too.

I wandered some way away from him and sat down on a rock to think. I was still thinking, fruitlessly, when I saw the *gig* coming around Droppy Nose Point and heading out to sea. Father was there – I recognised his cap. Old man Jenkins was in Billy's place and the chief was setting the jibsail. They were far too far away to see my turtle. I came back to him and sat down.

'See that *gig*?' I told him. 'One day I'm going to row in that *gig*, just like Billy did. One day.'

And I told him all about the *gig* and the big ships that come into Scilly needing a pilot to bring them in safely, and how the *gigs* race each other to get out there first. I told him about the wrecks too, and about how the *gigs* will put to sea in any weather if there's sailors to rescue or cargo to salvage. The strange thing is, I didn't feel at all silly talking to my turtle. I mean, I know it *is* silly, but it just seemed the natural thing to do. I honestly think I told the turtle more about me than I've ever told anyone before.

I looked down at him. He was nudging at the

sand with his chin, his mouth opening. He was hungry! I don't know why I hadn't thought of it before. I had no idea at all what turtles eat. So I tried what was nearest first - seaweed of all sorts, sea lettuce, bladderwrack, whatever I could find.

I dangled it in front of his mouth, brushing his nose with it so he could smell it. He looked as if he was going to eat it. He opened his mouth slowly and snapped at it. But then he turned his head away and let it fall to the ground.

'What then?' I asked.

A sudden shadow fell across me. Granny May was standing above me in her hat.

'How long have you been there?' I asked.

'Long enough,' she said and she walked around me to get a better look at the turtle.

'Let's try shrimps,' she said.

'Maybe he'll eat shrimps. We'd better hurry. We don't want anyone else finding him, do we?' And she sent me off home to fetch the shrimping net. I ran all the way there and all the way back, wondering if Granny May knew about her roof yet.

Granny May is the best shrimper on the island. She knows every likely cluster of seaweed on Rushy

Bay, and everywhere else come to that. One sweep through the shallows and she was back, her net jumping with shrimps. She smiled down at my turtle.

'Useful, that is,' she said, tapping him with her stick.

'What?' I replied.

'Carrying your house around with you. Can't hardly have your roof blowed off, can you?' So she did know.

'It'll mend,' she said. 'Roofs you can mend easily enough, hope is a little harder.'

She told me to dig out a bowl in the sand, right

under the turtle's chin, and then she shook out her net. He looked mildly interested for a moment and then looked away. It was no good. Granny May was looking out to sea, shielding her eyes against the glare of the sun.

'I wonder,' she murmured. 'I wonder. I shan't be long.' And she was gone, down to the sea. She was wading out up to her ankles, then up to her knees, her shrimping net scooping through the water around her. I stayed behind with the turtle and threw more stones at the gulls. When she came back, her net was bulging with jellyfish, blue jellyfish. She emptied them into the turtle's sandy bowl. At once he was at them like a vulture, snapping, crunching, swallowing, until there wasn't a tentacle left.

'He's smiling,' she said. 'I think he likes them. I think perhaps he'd like some more.'

'I'll do it,' I said. I picked up the net and rushed off down into the sea. They were not difficult to find. I've never liked jellyfish, not since I was stung on my neck when I was little and came out in a burning weal that lasted for months. So I kept a wary eye around me. I scooped up twelve big ones in as many minutes. He ate those and then lifted his head, asking for more. We took it in turns after that, Granny May and me, until at last he seemed to have had enough and left a half-chewed jellyfish lying there, the shrimps still hopping all around it. I crouched down and looked my turtle in the eye.

'Feel better now?' I asked, and I wondered if turtles burp when they've eaten too fast. He didn't burp, but he did move. The flippers dug deeper. He shifted - just a little at first. And then he was scooping himself slowly forward, inching his way through the sand. I went loony. I was cavorting up and down like a wild thing, and Granny May was just the same. The two of us whistled and whooped to keep him moving, but we knew soon enough that we didn't need to. Every step he took was stronger, his neck reaching forward purposefully. Nothing would stop him now. As he neared the sea, the sand was tide-ribbed and wet, and he moved ever faster, faster, past the rock pools and across the muddy sand where the lugworms leave their curly casts. His flippers were under the water now. He was half walking, half swimming. Then he dipped his snout into the sea and let the water run over his head and down his neck. He was going, and suddenly I didn't want him to. I was alongside him, bending over him.

'You don't have to go,' I said.

'He wants to,' said Granny May. 'He has to.'

He was in deeper water now, and with a few powerful strokes he was gone, cruising out through the turquoise water of the shallows to the deep blue beyond. The last I saw of him he was a dark shadow under the sea making out towards Samson.

I felt suddenly alone. Granny May knew it I think, because she put her arm around me and kissed the top of my head.

Back at home we never said a word about our turtle. It wasn't an arranged secret, nothing like that. We just didn't tell anyone because we didn't want to – it was private somehow.

Father says he'll try to make a start on her house tomorrow, just to keep out the weather. Granny May doesn't seem at all interested.

She just keeps smiling at me, confidentially. Mother knows something is going on between us, but she doesn't know what. I'd like to tell her, but I can't talk to her like I used to.

If Billy were here I'd tell him.

I haven't thought about Billy today and I should

have. All I've thought about is my turtle. If I don't think about Billy I'll forget him, and then it'll be as if he was never here at all, as if I never had a brother, as if he never existed, and if he never existed then he can't come back, and he must. He must.

This is the longest day I've ever written in my diary and all because of a turtle. My wrist aches.

OCTOBER 25TH

I LOVE THE SMELL OF PAINT IN THE SUNSHINE. Today we painted the gig outside the boathouse - Father and me together - and he began talking about Billy again. He's been talking more about him lately. I wish he wouldn't because he only ends up tormenting himself. Always the same impossible questions I can't answer: Why? Why did he go off like that? Where's he gone? Why doesn't he come home?

I just wish I had the courage to tell him, and to tell him straight: 'Because you would keep shouting at him, because he was sick of milking cows day in day out, sick of slaving on the farm every hour of every day.' But he wouldn't understand and it wouldn't do any good anyway. It wouldn't bring Billy back, would it?

We were painting all day. Mother and Granny May brought us out some bread and water and I sat down and admired the gig, sleek in the sun, a shining gleaming jet black. No one spoke.

When no one talks it means we're all thinking of Billy or of how long we can last out here on Bryher with the cows gone and no money coming in. When Granny May looks at me and smiles, I know she is thinking of our turtle.

I was looking out to sea today and I was thinking: they're out there, Billy and our turtle, both of them. Maybe one day our turtle will swim right underneath Billy's ship. They'll meet in mid-ocean and never know it. Maybe.

We finished painting the gig by sunset. A cold wind was getting up and my hands were numb. Everyone come down to the boathouse to look. The chief said how fine she looked and how she'd move faster through the water now she was painted. And I said she'd go a lot faster still if I rowed in her. They all laughed, but I wasn't joking. Father knew it. I caught his eye. He wasn't angry. I really think he was proud of me, just for a moment.

Mother looks so grey these days, and thin. She's always gazing out of the window. She's looking for Billy – I know she is, she's waiting for him. She and Father scarcely speak at all. Only Granny May talks and she talks more to herself than anyone else. I'm hungry. We're all hungry.

NOVEMBER 1ST

THE COLD OF WINTER HAS CREPT INTO THE house, into my room, into my bed. I curl up tight. I pile on blankets, but I cannot keep warm. Mother says I'm sickening for something.

Granny May stayed in her bed in Billy's room all day. She has a cough on her chest that won't leave her. When she's not coughing, there is a silence in the house that frightens me.

We had limpets for supper - again. There's little else to eat. I sleep a lot and drift from dream to dream. I dreamed of my turtle again today and I went in to tell Granny May. She's as white as her pillows. She smiled and said she can never remember her dreams. She said she'll be down again tomorrow, when she feels better. She's still cheerful - she's the only one of us that is. She looks older in bed. There's always a dew drop on the end of her nose. I try not to look at it. The house creaks in the wind, like a ship at sea. I am so cold.

NOVEMBER 30TH

WE ARE LEAVING. I READ IT AND I STILL CAN'T believe I am writing it. We are leaving Bryher for good, forever. And there's others doing the same thing, all over the island. Even the chief is leaving. I think that's maybe what finally made up Father's mind for him. He came out with it this evening.

'If he's going,' said Father, 'then that's an end of it, the end of Bryher, the end of us. There'll be no one left. We're leaving.'

'You can leave if you want to,' said Granny May quietly. 'But I'm staying put. 'You hear me? I'm staying put.'

Mother said what I was thinking. 'But what if

Billy comes back? We won't be here for him.'

Father spoke sharply without looking at her. 'We can't spend all our lives waiting for Billy,' he said. He didn't have to go off like he did, did he?'

Granny May took Mother's hands in hers.

'I'll be here,' she said. 'He'll find me and then he'll find you. He'll come back, you'll see.'

Mother looked at me and I tried all I could to give her some hope but she knew I was pretending.

She's sitting downstairs now, crushed and sunken in her chair. She doesn't cry and neither do I. My tears won't come because they don't want to come. The honest truth is that I want to leave. This house is full of sadness and hunger. We're lucky to have one meal a day. There's no bread, no milk, no eggs, only a few soft potatoes, and limpets – oh, there's always limpets. There's no joy, no laughter, no Billy.

No one smiles at you any more as you pass by, no one waves. Everywhere I see stooped figures bending into the wind, faces gaunt with hunger, yellow from too many limpets. Some people have left already. Sally and Sarah and all their family, and Mr and Mrs Gibson from the shop. Father says we'll be gone in a week or so – if the weather permits – on the next boat to the mainland. I shan't be sorry.

Granny May is sleeping in with me now. We try to keep each other warm. She's so thin. I've told her and I've told her she must come with us when we leave, but she won't listen. Instead, she whispers in the dark about our turtle. She wonders if we'd have done the same thing now, whether we'd have helped him back into the sea if we'd been as hungry as we are now. Granny May thinks we would, but I'm not so sure.

I can't sleep so I've lit the candle and am writing a bit more. More than anything I feel angry. Maybe that's why I can't sleep. I'm angry we're being driven out of our home, driven off our island, and angrier still that now I shall never be able to row in the gig . . .

Granny May has just woken up. She looked at me and said, 'I'm telling you, Laura, I am not leaving. You can write that down in your diary. I was born here. I'll die here. I'm not leaving.'

She's sleeping again now. When old people sleep, you can hardly see them breathe.

DECEMBER 6TH

WE'RE STILL HERE. THERE'VE BEEN STORMS for a week now. No one will be going anywhere till it's over. Granny May says it's an omen, a warning. The storm is telling us to stay, so we must stay. Father says he doesn't believe in omens and superstitions or any of that kind of thing, and they had a big argument. I've never heard Granny May so angry. She's made up her mind and she won't be gainsaid. She means it. She's set her heart on it. If she has her way no one will leave, and when Granny May sets her heart on something . . . maybe we won't be leaving after all.

Mother wants to stay too, but she says nothing.

She's disappeared inside herself completely, and I don't think she'll ever come out again, or smile, or laugh, or tell us everything will be all right, like she used to when Billy was here.

Sometimes now, I cannot picture Billy's face any more and I think maybe that's because he's dead. I don't want to think it, but I can't help myself.

DECEMBER 8TH

WILL THE RAIN NEVER STOP? WILL THE WIND blow forever? We hardly ever leave the house, just to cut limpets off the rocks and to bring in firewood from the shed. There's precious little wood left, and what there is, is damp.

Granny May won't eat. Mother has tried everything she can to tempt her - this evening the very last of the potatoes. She won't even look at it. She turns her face away, just like the turtle did. She'll die if she doesn't eat. She knows it and she doesn't care. And I know why. I really think she's made up her mind to die - that way at least she can stay here like she wants to.

She sleeps most of the time. She's sleeping now beside me and she's talking in her sleep, all about the turtle. I can't make any sense of it, but it's a kind of rambling prayer, not to God like prayers should be, but to the turtle. She's losing her mind, I think.

DECEMBER 9TH
The Wreck of the Zanzibar

I DON'T KNOW WHERE TO BEGIN. GRANNY MAY is still asleep. She wakes from time to time, and looks up at me fondly. I've told her again and again what's happened today. She just smiles and pats my hand. I hope she understands, but I'm not sure she does. I'm not sure I do.

Mother sent me out early as usual to fetch back some limpets or whatever I could find. It was too rough again to fish from the rocks. The storm was worse than ever. There must have been a dozen of us out doing the same thing on Great Porth, when someone saw the sail. The rain was coming in hail squalls, driving into my face so hard that I could scarcely open my eyes. One sail became four, white against the black storm clouds. The ship was beating her way past Seal Rock towards the Tearing Ledges, making no headway in the teeth of a gale. We all knew what was going to happen. We'd seen it before. A ship about to founder staggers before she falls. A huge wave broke over her stern and she did not come upright again. She lay on her side and wallowed in the waves.

The cry went up from all around. 'Wreck! Wreck!'

I raced home and met Father and the chief coming up the track at a run.

'Is it true?' cried Father. 'Have we got a wreck?'

When we reached the boathouse they were already hauling the gig down into the surf. Time and again, the crew leapt in and we pushed them out, up to our waists in the icy sea, and time and again they were driven back by the waves. In the end she was caught broadside on, capsized and everyone was upturned into the sea. After that everyone wanted to give up, everyone except the chief.

'Rushy Bay!' he cried. 'Nothing else for it. We'll be out of the wind. We'll launch her there!'

But no one would hear of it until the

schoolteacher came running along the beach towards us, breathless.

'There's men in the sea,' she said. 'I saw them from Samson Hill. The ship's gone on the rocks.'

'You heard her!' cried the chief. 'Well, what are we waiting for?'

They lashed the oars across, and at a word from the chief, lifted the gig up on to their shoulders. Mother was beside me now, taking my hand in hers, silent with anxiety. I stood and watched, yearning, aching to be carrying the gig, with the chief, with Father, with old man Jenkins and the others.

They staggered up the beach and set off across the Green towards Rushy Bay, all of us running alongside. When we reached the track up Samson Hill everyone made off up the hill to watch from the top, everyone but me. I stayed with the crew. Mother tried to hold on to me, but I broke free. Father bellowed at me, but I paid him no heed and I knew he was too busy to make me.

Over the dunes they went, cursing and groaning under the weight of the gig, and I went with them. And that was where Father went down with a cry, clutching at his ankle and rolling over in agony. When he tried to stand, he could not. I went to help him. He looked up, and shook his head.

'You take it!' the chief was shouting, and he was shouting at me. 'You, Laura, you!' He took me by the shoulders and shook me.

'Come on!'

So I took up Father's oar and my share of the weight on my shoulder, and leaving Father behind on the dunes, we ran the gig down the beach and into the sea. We unlashed our oars, leapt in, and at once we were pulling hard for Samson. The waves hurled us up and down so violently that I thought the gig would break her back.

I just rowed and as I rowed I suddenly realised where I was, and what I was doing. I was out in the gig! I was rowing out to a wreck! I was doing what I had always most wanted to do all my life. At last, at last, at last!

No one spoke except the chief. He stood in the prow bellowing at us.

'Row, you beggars, row. Row like hell. There's folk in the water out there. Row your hearts out. Row, blast your eyes, row!'

And I rowed like I had never rowed before, fixing my eyes on the blade, pulling long and hard through the water, reaching far forward, bracing my feet and digging the oar again into the sea. The sea surged and churned around the gig. I became my oar, my oar became me. I was too busy to feel any fear, too cold to feel any pain.

The gig grounded suddenly. I had not expected it so soon. We were on Samson already. We hung over our oars like wet rags, drained of all strength. But the chief hadn't finished with us yet.

'Out!' he cried, and he leapt over the side. 'We'll carry her across Samson and launch her again on the other side. It's the only way we'll reach them. Come on, you beggars. Be time to rest when it's done.'

So we tumbled over the side, lashed the oars again and lifted.

The neck of Samson is just a hundred yards or so across, but in the teeth of that gale, it felt like a mile. More than once I stumbled and fell to my knees, but always there were strong hands grasping me and hauling me to my feet.

'I can see them!' cried the chief. 'Over on White Island. I can see them.'

The chief was everywhere, lifting with us, bellowing behind us, clearing the way ahead of us. We reached the beach on the far side of Samson at last and ran the gig down over the pebbles until the sea took the weight of her from us. We unlashed the oars, pushed her out and piled in.

'Pull!' he cried. 'Pull for your children, pull for your wives.'

I have no children, I have no wife, but I pulled all the same. I pulled instead for Granny May, for Mother, for Father and for Billy, especially for Billy.

It was no great distance across the narrow channel but the seas were seething. A witches' brew of wind and tide and current took us and tossed us about at will. Under us the gig groaned and cried, but she held together. A thunderous wave reared up above us, a great green wall of water and I thought we must go over.

'Steady! Steady!' came the chief's voice, and even the wave seemed to obey him. I felt the boat rise with the wave, surge forward and then we were surfing in towards the beach where we were dumped high and safe on the shingle of White Island.

I climbed out and looked about me. I saw men staggering towards us, and one of them was running ahead of the others.

'Laura!' he cried. I knew the voice, and then I knew him.

'Billy?' I said, taking his face in my hands to be sure, to be quite sure. 'Is it you, Billy? Is it you?'

'Thank God,' he whispered.

I have to pinch myself still to believe it as I write it. Billy is back! Billy is safe! Billy is home! We hugged out there on White Island. We cried. We laughed.

On the way back to Bryher, with the wind and the waves behind us, with new strength in our arms, the gig flew over the sea. We had rescued every man

on board and Billy had come home. I could have rowed that *gig* single-handed.

They had hot baths ready all over the island. Billy sat there, laughing in the tub in the kitchen with all of us around, and shivered the cold out of him.

He was bigger, stronger, different somehow, but still Billy. We had hot soup – limpets again – but we didn't care, not now. I've never seen anyone as hungry.

I've never seen Mother glowing so, nor Father so

motherly. Everyone's proud of me. I'm proud of me. Billy's too tired to talk much, he says his ship was called the *Zanzibar.* She was bound for New York from France. He was suddenly tired and Mother took him up to bed. He'll tell us more tomorrow.

I've just told Granny May again that Billy's back home, but all she says is: 'The turtle, the turtle.'

She's asleep again now. I am so tired and I am so happy.

DECEMBER 10TH

WHEN I WOKE UP THIS MORNING I THOUGHT yesterday must be a dream. I had to go into Billy's room to be quite sure it wasn't. He was still asleep. He sleeps like a baby, like he always did, with his finger alongside his nose.

The wind has dropped. From his window I watched the sea dancing in the morning light. Father was on his way out when I got downstairs, leaning on a stick and limping, but beaming at me.

'The *Zanzibar,*' he said, 'she's still on the rocks – what's left of her. But she won't be there for long. We're going out to see what we can take off.'

Mother tried to stop him but he wouldn't listen.

I tried to go with him but Mother wouldn't have it. She stood between me and the door, took hold of me and sat me down firmly.

Later on, I went up Samson Hill with Mother, leaving Billy and Granny May still asleep. Every boat from Bryher was out around White Island. The wreck was high on the rocks, only her prow hidden under the water, her sails were in tatters. There were men crawling all over her like ants. As we watched we saw the gig pulling slowly away from White Island. She was low in the water. There was laughter across the sea.

As the gig came into Rushy Bay below us, I saw something lashed to either side of her. Mother could not make out what it was and neither could I. The crew shipped their oars some way from shore and let the gig come in slowly on her own. Then I saw the chief and old man Jenkins leaning out over the side. They had knives in their hands and they were cutting at the ropes.

'Cows!' someone said. And at that moment, amid great splashing and whooping from the gig, six cows came out of the sea and came gambolling up the beach.

'Well, I'll be beggared,' said Mother.

The crew leapt out after them, and then began a great cow chase all over Rushy Bay, Father waving his stick at everyone and shouting. In the end it was difficult to say who was chasing who. We all ran down Samson Hill to help, and drove them up over the dunes on to the Green where they settled at last to graze. Father, all breathless, leaned on his stick and shook his head.

'Well,' he said. 'Would you believe it?'

But there was a lot more than cows on the wreck of the *Zanzibar.* All afternoon the boats came back and forth loaded to the gunnels with timber, with corn, and with brandy! Billy was up by now, and along with all the other rescued sailors from the *Zanzibar,* he lent a hand.

By this evening, the beach on Rushy Bay was littered with piles of loot – every family had their own pile and we ferried it all back home in donkey carts.

We had prayed for a wreck and a wreck had come. And what a wreck! That a miracle had happened, no one doubts. There is wood enough to rebuild our battered houses, and to rebuild or replace our ruined boats. There are cows to give us milk, all the corn we need to feed us and them through the winter, and there'll be enough over for seed next spring. And brandy enough, Father says, to keep us all happy forever.

Granny May insisted we get her up. She keeps touching Billy to be sure he's real. She took some soup - the first time she'd eaten for days - and then made us take her to Rushy Bay to see the wreck. She couldn't walk, so Billy and his friends from the *Zanzibar* pulled her across the island in the back of a cart, as the donkeys were still busy. She was beside me this evening, at high tide, when we heard the *Zanzibar* groan. Everyone was there to watch her go. We watched her sink slowly into the sea, her shredded sails whipping in the wind, waving at us. I waved back in silence. The crew took off their hats, some crossed themselves and one of them fell on his knees in the sand and thanked God. And then we all knelt with him, except Granny May, I noticed.

We're staying. Everyone's staying. Billy's staying. He's said so, he promised. He's crossed his heart and hoped to die. He's been all over the world - America, Ireland, France, Spain, Africa even. Imagine that, Africa. I asked about Joseph Hannibal. It seems he didn't quite turn out as Billy had expected.

He drank a lot. He borrowed Billy's money and never gave it back. And when Billy asked for it, he threatened him. So Billy left the *General Lee* in New York and became a cabin-boy on the *Zanzibar.* It was the *Zanzibar* that had taken him all over the world.

Billy says there are beautiful places in the world,

wonders you wouldn't believe unless you saw them with your own eyes, but that there's nowhere else in the world quite like Scilly, nowhere like home. I told him I knew that already, and Father said there's some things you've got to find out for yourself, and Billy and he smiled at each other.

DECEMBER 24TH

I'M MILKING THE *ZANZIBAR* COWS, AND WITH Billy, too. Three of the six are in milk and we think the others may be in calf – let's hope! Everyone had most of what they want off the wreck. There's been some grumbles, of course, but it's been fair shares. We've got the cows because we're the only ones who know how to handle them – we got some corn, too – everyone did. We've rebuilt the cowshed just as it was. Granny May has enough wood for her roof. There's timber stacked up in gardens all over the island. There's boats being mended, roofs going on. Everyone, everywhere, is hammering and sawing. Bryher is alive again.

Granny May will probably be with us until the spring, till her house is ready. She's the same now as she ever was, scuttling about the place and muttering to herself. Sometimes I think she is the 'mad old stick' everyone says she is. She keeps telling me it wasn't God that brought the wreck that brought Billy back to us, it was the turtle. She rambles on and on about how there's no such thing as a miracle. If something happens, then something has made it happen. Law of nature, she says. We saved the turtle and so the turtle saved us. It's that simple. You get what you deserve in this world, she says. I don't know that she's right.

I've told Billy all about the turtle. He says if he'd found it, he'd have eaten it, but he wouldn't have. He's just saying that. We talk and we talk. We've hardly stopped talking since he came back. I've heard his stories over and over, but I want to hear them again and again. I know them so well, it's as if I was with him all the time he was away, as if I've been to America and Africa, as if I've seen for myself the great cities, the deserts that go on forever and icebergs and mountains that reach up and touch the sky.

The crew of the *Zanzibar* left from the quay this

evening. We were there to wave them off. Everyone hugged everyone. They were all so happy to be alive and so grateful to us for saving them.

Since he's been back, Billy hasn't had a cross word with Father, and Mother is my mother again.

DECEMBER 25TH
Christmas Day

IT SEEMS GRANNY MAY MIGHT HAVE BEEN right after all. I was with Billy cleaning out the cowshed after church when he called me outside. Everyone seemed to be running down towards Green Bay and there was a crowd gathered down on the beach. So we left everything and ran. We met Mother and Granny May coming out of the house.

'There's been a dead turtle washed up,' said Mother. Granny May looked at me, her eyes full of tears. We had to push through the crowd. People were laughing, and I hated them for that. He was covered in sand and seaweed and they were trying to roll him over, but he was too heavy, even for them.

Then I looked *again*. It was *a* turtle all right, but it was not our turtle. It wasn't any turtle at all. It was painted bright green with yellow eyes and it looked as if it had been carved out of wood. It was the figurehead off a ship.

Billy crouched down beside it, and brushed the sand off its face.

'That's off the *Zanzibar,*' he said.

Granny May was laughing through her tears. She took my hand and squeezed it.

'Now do you believe me?' she said, and she didn't need an answer.

'If it's off Billy's ship,' she went on, 'then it belongs to Billy, doesn't it?' No one argued with her.

'We'll call him Zanzibar and he can live in the garden. Let's get him home.' So we heaved him up on to a cart and trundled him home. All afternoon we scrubbed. A lot of his paint had come off in the sea. He's a little bigger than our turtle was but his face is just the same, wizened, wrinkled and wise like a two hundred year old man. And he smiles just the same too – gently.

I'm looking out of my window as I write this. He looks as if he's trying to eat the grass. He won't, of course. He'll only eat jellyfish. Zanzibar is a good name for him, the right name, I think.

(On the last page, she had written in ink, in the wobbly handwriting of an old lady:)

P.S. One Last Thing

I'm not leaving Zanzibar to anyone. I'm leaving him to everyone. So I want him put out on the Green so all the children of Bryher can sit on him whenever they like. They can ride him wherever they like. He can be a horse, a dragon, a dolphin, an elephant or even a leatherback turtle.

As you know, your Great-uncle Billy lived a good long life. When he died, I didn't know how I'd manage without him. But I did, because I had to. Anyway, we're together again now.

L.P. 1995

MARZIPAN

I SAT THERE ON THE BED FOR SOME MOMENTS, looking at the last of Great-aunt Laura's drawings – of Zanzibar on the Green gazing out to sea. Sitting astride him is a small girl. The wind is in her hair and she's laughing out of sheer joy.

From outside the window I heard peals of laughter. I leaned out. There must have been half a dozen little nieces and nephews down in the garden and clambering all over Zanzibar. The smallest of them, Catherine it was – my youngest niece, was offering Zanzibar some grass and stroking his head between his eyes.

'Come on, Marzipan,' she was saying, 'you'll like it.'

'He won't eat it,' I called down. 'He only eats jellyfish.' She looked up at me, squinting into the sun.

'How do you know?' she asked.

'If you let me sit on him,' I said, 'I'll tell you. I'll tell you where Zanzibar came from, how he got here, everything.'

'All right,' she said.

So, sitting on Zanzibar in the evening sun, I read them Great-aunt Laura's diary from beginning to end. By the time I'd finished, the entire family was gathered around Zanzibar and listening.

I closed the book. 'That's it,' I said. No one spoke for some time.

It was Catherine's idea that we should move Zanzibar right away. So we fetched Great-aunt Laura's rickety cart out of her shed, loaded up Zanzibar and hauled him along the rutty track to the Green. I knew from that last drawing in the diary exactly where she wanted him put. And that's where we left him, gazing out to sea.

When I looked back there were gulls circling above him. Some had landed on his back, and one on his head. Catherine was running at them, waving her hands and shouting. 'Shoo!' she cried. 'Shoo!' They flew off, protesting; and Catherine caught us up.

'Anyway, it doesn't matter, does it?' she said. 'They can't eat him, can they? Marzipan's made of wood, isn't he?'

'Zanzibar,' I said. 'He's called Zanzibar.'

'That's what I said,' she replied, and skipped off after the others.

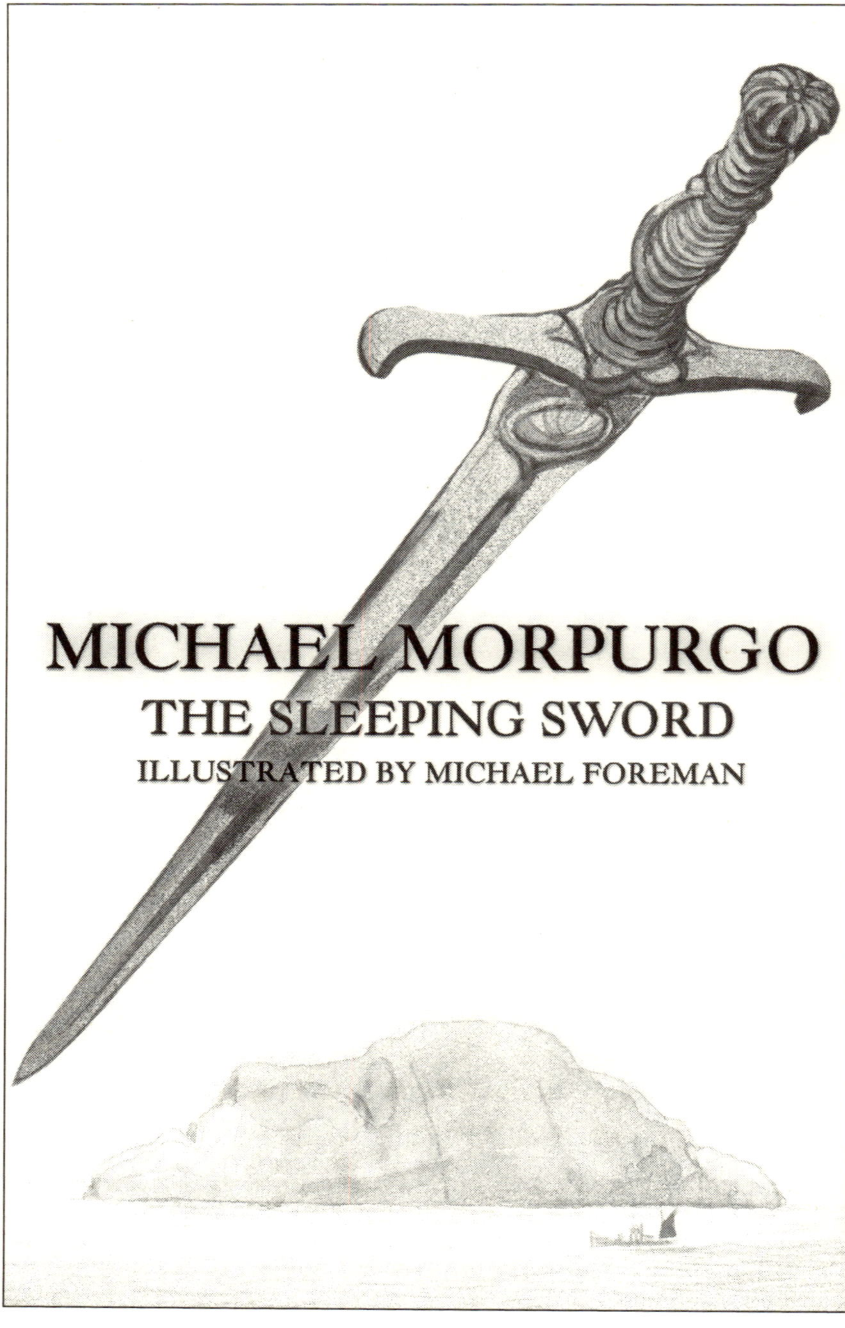
MICHAEL MORPURGO
THE SLEEPING SWORD
ILLUSTRATED BY MICHAEL FOREMAN

The magic of King Arthur continues . . .

THE SLEEPING SWORD

MICHAEL MORPURGO

ILLUSTRATED BY MICHAEL FOREMAN

I felt all around me. On every side there were earth walls. In a panic, I groped above me for the hole I must have fallen through. I tried again and again to haul myself up, but the soil roof kept giving way and falling in on me. I must have been aware of the rumble of the tractor, but only now did I realise that it was close and coming closer, that it was heading straight for me.

Bun Bendle stumbles one day into an underground tomb containing a shield and a beautiful, ancient sword. As he touches the hilt, his whole body is gripped by an incredible, centuries-old power. It is a power that will change Bun's life for ever.